THE AMERICAN GIRLS

 1764 KAYA, an adventurous Nez Perce girl whose deep love for horses and respect for nature nourish her spirit

 1774 FELICITY, a spunky, spritely colonial girl, full of energy and independence

 1824 JOSEFINA, a Hispanic girl whose heart and hopes are as big as the New Mexico sky

 1854 KIRSTEN, a pioneer girl of strength and spirit who settles on the frontier

 1864 ADDY, a courageous girl determined to be free in the midst of the Civil War

 1904 SAMANTHA, a bright Victorian beauty, an orphan raised by her wealthy grandmother

 1934 KIT, a clever, resourceful girl facing the Great Depression with spirit and determination

 1944 MOLLY, who schemes and dreams on the home front during World War Two

 1974 JULIE, a fun-loving girl from San Francisco who faces big changes—and creates a few of her own.

1974
HAPPY NEW YEAR,
Julie

By MEGAN McDONALD

ILLUSTRATIONS ROBERT HUNT

VIGNETTES SUSAN McALILEY

★ American Girl®

Printed in China
07 08 09 10 11 12 LEO 10 9 8 7 6 5 4 3 2 1

PICTURE CREDITS
The following individuals and organizations have generously given
permission to reprint images contained in "Looking Back":
p. 19—Fairmont Image Gallery (Fairmont hotel); p. 65—Better Homes and Gardens (decorating
tree); pp. 66-67—Getty Images (kids); Better Homes and Gardens (ornaments);
© Phil Schermeister/Corbis (Flower Fair); Corbis (calligraphy practice); © Phil Schermeister/
Corbis (cookie factory); © Lawrence Migdale/www.migdale.com (New Year dinner); pp. 68-69—
© Robert Holmes/Corbis (girls in parade); © Lawrence Migdale/www.migdale.com (dragon).

Cataloging-in-Publication Data available from the Library of Congress.

FOR LOUISE, ANNIE,
AND ELIZA

TABLE OF CONTENTS

JULIE'S FAMILY AND FRIENDS

JULIE'S FAMILY

JULIE
*A girl full of energy
and new ideas, trying to
find her place in
times of change*

TRACY
*Julie's trendy
teenage sister, who is
fifteen years old*

MOM
*Julie's artistic
mother, who runs
a small store*

DAD
*Julie's father,
an airline pilot who flies
all over the world*

IVY
Julie's best friend,
who loves doing
gymnastics

CHAPTER
ONE

CHANGES FOR
CHRISTMAS

Julie stepped inside a forest of
evergreen. The spicy scent of pine
tickled her nose. The hum of traffic,
honking of horns, and barking of dogs faded as a
hush fell over her. Closing her eyes, Julie imagined
standing in the middle of a pine forest . . . the
Christmas-tree farm up north near her grandparents'
house. "Too small," "Too crooked," "Too scraggly,"
they'd say, searching for the perfect tree. And
Grandma would bring hot chocolate in a thermos . . .

"Julie! Over here!" A man's voice called her
back to the present—the Christmas-tree lot on the
corner of San Francisco's Ashbury and Waller streets.
"Hey! Are you my first customers?" It was Hank,

1

a friend from the neighborhood.

"I wish," said Julie's older sister, Tracy. "We were on our way to the bakery when Julie gave all her money to the Salvation Army."

"Just what was in my change purse," said Julie. "I didn't have enough for a Christmas tree anyway."

"Mom and Dad used to take us up to Santa Rosa every year to a Christmas-tree farm near our grandma and grandpa's," Tracy explained.

"And you cut down your own tree!" Julie gushed. "And there's a train you can ride, and you get free apple crisp, and—"

"But not this year," said Tracy, kicking at a stone with her boot. "Mom says money's tight and she has to work around the clock."

"And since we're spending Christmas at Dad's, she says we don't need a tree this year," Julie added glumly. A few months ago, Mom and Dad had divorced, and Julie and Tracy now split their time between the apartment and their old house, where Dad lived.

"How would you girls like to *adopt* a tree for Christmas?" Hank disappeared behind a row of trees. He came out pulling a red wagon that held a perfectly plump tree in a redwood planter, with feathery branches like arms reaching to the sky.

"I bought a live tree to plant outside the Veterans' Center. We could really use some *sprucing* up over there," Hank said with a wink. "You're welcome to take the tree home until I have time to plant it. It'll last indoors for a week or two."

"Really? You mean it?" Julie asked.

"Scout's honor," said Hank, holding up three fingers. "It's ready to go. All you have to do is water it."

"It's perfect," said Tracy.

"Thanks, Hank," said Julie.

❁

The two sisters stepped back to admire the tree that now filled the second-story bay window at the front of the apartment.

"C'mon," said Tracy. "Let's get out the decorations. We can have this tree sparkling before Mom gets done at the shop." It was Mom's first Christmas season at Gladrags, the store she owned downstairs on the first floor of their apartment building, and the holiday shoppers were keeping her busy.

"I don't know where Mom put all the Christmas stuff after the move," said Julie. "Do you?"

Tracy shook her head. "I'll go down and ask her."

"No, wait! Then she'll know—"

"Know what?" asked Mom, coming up the stairs.

"Aw," said Julie. "We got a tree from Hank, and we were going to surprise you and decorate it so that you wouldn't have to go to any trouble."

"But we couldn't find the ornaments," Tracy added.

"Tell you what," said Mom. "Let's all decorate the tree tonight, after I close up. It'll be fun. But right now, I'm really swamped with customers. Can you two give me a hand?"

"Sure, I can run the cash register," said Tracy.

"And I could gift-wrap," said Julie.

"Fantastic," said Mom. "With your help, I won't have to turn into a grinch after all."

"What a day!" said Mom as Tracy finally flipped the sign on the front door to CLOSED. "I still have to count the money. Why don't you girls go on upstairs and think about what to have for supper."

4

"Grilled cheese!" said Julie.

"And tomato soup," said Tracy. "We'll make it, Mom."

"Then we decorate," said Julie.

As soon as the supper dishes were cleared, Julie asked again about the ornaments. Mom frowned and thought for a moment, then looked up sheepishly. "I just remembered—when we moved, I knew we had a lot less storage space here, so I left the Christmas stuff at Dad's."

"What are we gonna do?" asked Julie. "We have this beautiful tree and no ornaments." She lightly touched the tip of one of the branches. "Hey, wait, I know. We could make our own ornaments."

"But we don't even have lights or tinsel or anything," said Tracy.

"We can string popcorn," Mom suggested.

"I guess," Tracy said skeptically. "But what about Grandma's old-fashioned teapot ornament? And the hummingbird with the fancy wings? It doesn't seem like Christmas without those."

"Yeah, and don't forget the green glass pickle you hide every year, Mom," said Julie.

"I like your idea of making ornaments," Mom said.

"Well, I could fold some origami paper cranes," said Julie. "We learned how in school."

Mom smiled and nodded. "Tracy, what about those god's eyes you made out of yarn and chopsticks? They'd brighten up any tree."

origami cranes

"Mom, I made those in Girl Scouts a hundred million years ago," Tracy grumbled.

"But they're really neat," said Julie. "Let's get them." She darted from room to room, collecting things to hang on the tree—a string of bells, a pincushion heart, Tracy's colorful god's eyes.

god's eye

"Tracy, why don't you get the popcorn popping on the stove, and I'll put on some Christmas music," Mom said.

"All the records are at Dad's, too," said Tracy.

"Then how about your transistor radio?" Mom suggested. "I'm sure we can find a station that plays Christmas music."

Soon Mom was humming "Deck the Halls" and even Tracy got into the spirit, stringing the popcorn. Julie folded origami cranes, and Tracy attached thread for hanging. Then Julie and Mom got busy with construction paper and scissors, making a paper chain that snaked across the coffee table, over the

*Julie and Mom made a paper chain that snaked across the coffee table,
over the beanbag chair, and down the hall.*

beanbag chair, and out into the hall. Mom even showed them how to melt crayons in wax paper with the iron to make ornaments that looked like stained glass.

Finally Mom let out a yawn and ran fingers through her hair. "We don't have to finish it all tonight, you know," she said.

"Are you kidding?" said Julie. "This is better than Santa's workshop!"

Mom smiled. "Well, it's past eleven—I think Santa's workshop is closed for the evening."

❁

On Christmas Eve, while Mom closed the shop, Tracy made tacos and Julie melted chocolate in a pan for her favorite dessert—chocolate fondue. As soon as Tracy had dipped the last strawberry into the gooey mixture, Julie started to pass out gifts from under the tree.

"I made all my presents," she said, handing a box to Tracy. "Hope you like this."

Tracy ripped off the wrapping paper. Inside was a denim cover for her tennis racket sewn from an old pair of jeans and decorated with a patchwork daisy.

"You made this?" said Tracy, her face lighting up. "Groovy! Thanks, Jules."

After opening presents, they sat quietly in the half-dark by the glow of the fireplace. Julie gazed at the flickering blue flames licking the logs. She longed to be filled with the spirit of Christmas, but instead of feeling joyous, she felt strangely hollow.

"It doesn't feel like Christmas Eve," she said quietly.

Mom reached over and brushed back Julie's hair. "We had a long day," Mom said. "Why don't we all head to bed. Dad'll be here first thing in the morning."

Julie looked at her small pile of gifts—the knitting kit from Tracy, the macramé belt and embroidered peasant shirt from Mom. Something was missing, and it wasn't presents.

"I miss Grandma and Grandpa, and driving up to the farm on Christmas Eve, and going caroling . . ." Julie let out a shaky sigh. She didn't add that she missed having Dad there, too.

"I know," Mom said in a thin voice, rubbing her forehead. "Believe me, I'd love nothing more than being with both of you at Grandma and Grandpa's for Christmas. But we have to be fair to Dad, too, and just accept that—"

"—'things are different this year,'" Tracy mimicked.

Mom shot her a sharp look. "Bedtime," she said again.

✿

"Hey!" said Julie. "You almost spit toothpaste on me." The two girls leaned over the sink, brushing their teeth.

"Well, I'm mad enough to spit," said Tracy, putting the cap back onto the toothpaste tube with an extra-hard twist. "I don't care what Mom says. I'm not going to Dad's."

"But you have to come. Besides, Mom's going to Grandma and Grandpa's in Santa Rosa. You can't just stay here all by yourself."

"I don't care. I'm not going, and they can't make me."

Climbing into bed, Julie hunkered down under the covers. But the warm quilt was no comfort tonight. She missed Nutmeg, her pet rabbit, who lived at Dad's. Julie kicked at the twisted covers. The hall clock chimed midnight, but she couldn't get Tracy's words out of her mind.

Padding barefoot down the hall to Tracy's room, she stood in the doorway a moment before asking softly, "Tracy? You asleep?"

"Yes," said Tracy.

"Can I come in?"

"Mm-hmm," Tracy grunted. Julie took that as a yes.

"I can't sleep," said Julie.

"What's wrong?" asked Tracy, lifting up the comforter and scooting over to make a space for her sister. Julie slid into the warm bed and propped her head up on one elbow.

"Tracy," Julie started, "you just have to come to Dad's tomorrow. It won't be Christmas without you."

Tracy sighed. "C'mon, Jules. You go to Dad's lots of weekends without me. It'll be fine."

"This is different," said Julie. "It's already going to be hard enough without Mom there. But it'll be twice as bad without you."

"I'm not going to get any more beauty sleep until we talk about this, am I?" Tracy asked. Julie shook her head. Tracy propped up her pillows and leaned against the back of the bed. "This has nothing to do with

you, Jules. I want us to be together, too. But everything's changed with the divorce. All my friends are
here now. There's nothing for me at Dad's anymore."

"There's Dad! What about him?" Julie asked,
tears stinging the corners of her eyes.

"Well, if Dad misses me, then it's his fault for
getting divorced. If he didn't want to be apart from
us, then how come we had to move out?"

Julie squeezed her eyes shut against the slow,
leaking tears. "It'll be so lonely with just me and Dad."

Tracy wiped Julie's cheek with the soft flannel of
her pajama sleeve. "Don't cry, Jules. C'mon. If it
means this much to you, I'll come with you to Dad's
tomorrow, for Christmas."

"Really?" Julie looked up through her tears.

"Yes," said Tracy, pulling the comforter up snug
under Julie's chin. "Okay? Merry Christmas. Now,
please let me get some sleep."

Julie turned onto her side, snuggling next to her
sister. "Merry Christmas," she whispered.

12

CHAPTER
TWO

PROBLEMS AND
PUZZLES

Saying good-bye to Mom on Christmas
morning was even harder than Julie had
imagined. She waved through the back
window all the way down Redbud Street until Dad
rounded the corner onto Haight Street. Finally, she
turned and faced forward. She missed Mom already,
but she was determined to make this a merry
Christmas anyway.

Twinkling lights twined around lampposts
up and down Haight Street, and psychedelic
wreaths adorned the front doors of shops, lifting
her spirits. Julie pointed out the funny wreaths to
Tracy. But Tracy just kept turning the radio dial
back and forth.

"Find some Christmas carols," said Julie. "We can sing along."

"We don't need the radio," said Dad, breaking into a verse of "Rudolph the Red-Nosed Reindeer." Julie joined in wholeheartedly.

"Oh brother," Tracy groaned.

As they turned onto their old street in North Beach, Julie hugged herself in anticipation. She pictured the Christmas candles glowing in the windows of their old house, the front door wrapped in foil like a giant gift, the mountain of presents tucked under the sparkling tree. But when she dashed up the steps to the house, no candles glowed in the windows and only the plain, dull door greeted her, stiff and wooden. Then she realized that it was Mom who always wrapped the door.

"Dad, where are the candles?" Julie asked.

"And where's the tree?" Tracy asked, pointing to the bare spot in the living room.

"Hold your horses," said Dad. "Don't worry. It's in the den this year."

Julie made her way through the house, feeling like a visiting stranger. In the den, a small three-foot tree sat on the corner end table. It had a few blinking lights, a handful of ornaments, and some tinsel.

"That's it?" asked Tracy.

"Fake?" Julie couldn't help exclaiming. "You got us a fake tree?" She touched one of the plastic branches. "It doesn't even smell like Christmas!"

"C'mon, it's not so bad, is it? Think of all the work we saved, not having to mess with all those needles that get into the carpet."

Julie collapsed into a chair, trying to swallow her disappointment. She picked at a tiny hole in her corduroys. The rip just grew larger.

"We've got cookies," said Dad, sounding a little too jolly. "Homemade! Why don't I get us all cookies and milk, and then we can start opening presents."

Julie jumped up and ran outside to the hutch to get Nutmeg. She came back holding her rabbit close, stroking Nutmeg's fluffy coat and floppy ears. Tracy sat stiffly on a footstool, gazing out the window with her back to the blinking tree.

"C'mon, Tracy. I'm disappointed too," Julie whispered. "But Dad's trying really hard. He baked cookies and everything."

Tracy shrugged. "Big deal. It's not like we're five, and cookies and milk will make everything better."

"It's Dad's first Christmas without Mom, too, you know," said Julie. "Can't you just try and make the best of it?"

"Shh. Here he comes," Tracy mouthed.

"Here we are!" said Dad, sporting a red Santa hat with white fur trim. "Take your pick." He held out a tin with layers of sugar-dusted Christmas cookies. "We have stars, trees, snowmen, you name it."

"These look great, Dad! I didn't know you knew how to bake cookies," said Julie.

"Actually," said Dad, chuckling, "Mrs. Martinelli next door brought them over this morning. Okay, girls, who wants to open the first present?"

"Me!" said Julie as Dad tossed her a shiny red box wrapped with a big bow.

In no time, the room was littered with Christmas wrappings. Nutmeg scampered around the den, burrowing under piles of wrapping paper. Julie bent over the pages of a new Nancy Drew mystery from Dad called *The Secret of the Forgotten City*.

"Thanks, Dad," said Julie. "This is the new one! I can't wait to read it."

Tracy reached over and stuck a tangled clump of

stray tinsel on top of Julie's head. "And I can't wait till you see yourself in the mirror!" Tracy said, pointing to Julie's hair.

Julie grinned. She didn't care how silly she looked—Tracy was actually smiling for the first time that morning.

Tracy tore off the wrapping from her last present and let out a whoop. "Dad! I can't believe it—a princess phone! This is exactly what I wanted. Far out!" She held up a bubble-gum-pink telephone. "And it even has a light-up dial. How did you know, Dad?"

Dad smiled. "Your mom told me how much you wanted one."

"Yeah, because at home, she's always scolding me for stretching the phone cord down the hall to my room. Now I'll be able to call my friends on my very own phone," Tracy exclaimed.

"Can I run across the street and show Ivy my new charm bracelet?" Julie asked Dad.

"You'll have plenty of time for Ivy later," said Dad. "You'll be here a whole week. But today is our day to be together as a family."

"I know," said Julie, "let's play one of my new board games. How about Clue?

"Great idea!" said Dad.

"Do I have to play?" Tracy asked.

"We could watch a Christmas program," said Dad. "I bet *The Grinch* is on today."

"Or *A Charlie Brown Christmas*," said Julie.

"Cartoons? I'm in high school now," Tracy grumbled.

Julie sighed. No matter what they suggested, it wouldn't be right. Why did Tracy have to be in one of her teenage moods on Christmas? "Well, what's something you want to do, Tracy?" Julie asked.

"You guys go ahead and play a game," Tracy said with a weak smile. "I'll just listen to the radio and read my new paperback."

Julie looked at Dad and shrugged. "Well, okay," said Dad. "Maybe just one game. Later we'll think of something that will be fun for all of us."

"I call Mrs. Peacock!" said Julie, setting up the Clue game.

Tracy curled up in the overstuffed chair by the window, put the earpiece in her ear, and fiddled with the dial on her transistor.

Julie tried keeping her mind on Clue, but she couldn't help wondering why Tracy wouldn't play a game with them. Was she mad that Julie had talked her into coming to Dad's for Christmas?

After the second game, Dad rubbed his hands together and asked, "Anyone else getting chilly in here? Who wants to help build a fire?"

"Me!" said Julie. Tracy looked up but didn't budge from her comfy chair.

"Julie, grab some old newspapers, okay?"

Julie crumpled newspaper, tossing it in with the kindling. "Hey, look at this," she said, pointing to an ad in the paper. "They have a Nutcracker Tea at this fancy hotel for Christmas."

"The Fairmont Hotel," said Dad, reading over her shoulder. "That's in Nob Hill. It has some of the best views in the city."

Fairmont Hotel   *Maybe this would help lift Tracy's spirits,* Julie thought. *Who wouldn't like dressing up and spending Christmas afternoon at a fancy hotel?* A small fizz of excitement bubbled up inside her. She'd been feeling bad about forcing Tracy to come, but this would make up for it.

"Dad? Could we go to the Nutcracker Tea? We could ride a cable car. They're all decorated for the holidays. One even has a Christmas tree on top!"

"Sounds good to me," said Dad. "This looks like something we'd all enjoy."

White lights twinkled like stars along the entrance to the Fairmont. Julie felt like a princess on her way to the palace as she stepped off the red-carpet walkway and into a grand room filled with gold-veined pillars, a marble floor, and an ornate gilded ceiling.

"Wow," said Julie, twirling around. "I've never seen such a fancy place." She was glad she'd packed her best outfit, a cranberry red velvet jumper, and pleased to have such a pretty place to wear it. Even Tracy seemed impressed with all the finery.

Giant spruce trees rimmed the main lobby. Julie, Tracy, and Dad made their way slowly around the room, stopping to admire each tree. The first was hung with Russian nesting dolls of all sizes. The next was lit with Chinese lanterns and silk fans.

"Ivy would love this Chinese tree," said Julie.

"And look at this one with toy nutcrackers."

"This one has sugarplum fairies," said Tracy. "They're so pretty."

"I get it!" said Julie. "Each tree is part of the Nutcracker story—like the ballet we went to last year. Remember?" Tracy nodded, her eyes flickering with wonder. Dad beamed.

When they were finished gazing at the trees, Dad ushered them into the hotel restaurant. They sat at a table beneath a glass-domed rotunda, with plush velvet seats and crystal water glasses. Even the napkins were folded into fancy swans.

"Do we have to drink tea?" asked Tracy.

"Can we order hot chocolate?" asked Julie.

"Three hot chocolates, coming right up," said Dad. The hot chocolate was served in delicate china cups, heaped with mountains of whipped cream.

"Look, the stirrer is a candy cane!" said Julie.

"This calls for a toast," Dad said, raising his cup. "Here's to being together for Christmas!" Julie raised her cup, too, clinking it with Dad's. Tracy just sat, stirring her hot chocolate into a whirlpool.

Dad waited awkwardly, his cup still half lifted in the air.

"C'mon, Tracy," Julie urged. "Clink your teacup!"

Tracy stared at the table. "I promised I'd come for Christmas, but one day together doesn't magically make us a family again."

"We *are* a family, honey," Dad said gently.

Julie sucked in a breath. "Tracy, you act like Dad divorced *us!*"

"Well, it feels like he divorced me," Tracy said, her voice starting to wobble. "You don't even know me anymore, Dad. Ever since we had to move out, it's like you don't even care about me."

"Tracy, honey, you know that's not true." Dad

reached out to tenderly squeeze Tracy's hand. She pulled it back, as if she'd been stung.

"You don't understand me at all!" Tracy said, choking back tears as she slid out of the booth, knocking over a crystal water glass.

Julie's mouth hung open. Dad stood and reached out to give Tracy a hug, but she jerked free and stormed out of the restaurant. Dad and Julie followed.

In the middle of the sidewalk, right in front of the Fairmont Hotel, Tracy covered her face with her hands, heaving with sobs. Dad put his arms around her shoulders, and this time she didn't pull away.

As soon as they got home, Tracy made a beeline for her room.

Dad stopped her on the stairs. "Tracy, I know you're upset, but I just want to say one thing. I love you and want to be part of your life. But you have to let me. So when you're ready, I'll be right here. I'll always be here for you."

Tracy turned and headed back up the stairs without a word. Julie started after her. But Dad caught her up in a hug.

"Let her go, honey," Dad said. "She just needs a little time."

"But I don't understand. One minute everything's fine, and the next she's crying and running out of the restaurant."

"I know, honey. She's just hurting. Tracy and I have been apart since the divorce, and we need to find a way back to each other." Dad gave Julie a comforting squeeze and said, "Now, you and I could use a little holiday cheer. What do you say we start that new thousand-piece puzzle Santa brought?"

"Sure, Dad," said Julie, showing him a shaky smile.

Julie sorted out the edge pieces and lined them up, trying to make sense of her jumbled feelings. *If only feelings were as simple to sort out as a jigsaw puzzle,* she thought with a sigh.

 The morning after Christmas, Julie woke up to birdsong in the bamboo hedges outside her window. She rubbed a swash through the fog on the window and peered

across the street. Ivy's curtains were open and her cats, Won Ton and Jasmine, were sunning in the window. That meant Ivy was up. Julie threw on her corduroys and her new peasant shirt from Mom, gobbled down a muffin, left a note for Dad, and hurried across the street.

Ivy opened the front door, holding her little sister by the hand. Missy had purple jelly all over her mouth.

"Hi, Joo-hee," said Missy. At three, she still had trouble with Julie's name.

"Hi, Missy Mouse," said Julie. "Merry Christmas," she said, handing Ivy a present.

"Thanks!" said Ivy. "C'mon in. Your present's still under the tree."

 Julie slipped off her shoes—a tradition at Ivy's house. She wiggled her toes into a pair of Chinese silk slippers by the front door as Won Ton and Jasmine rubbed against her ankles.

In the front room, Ivy's twelve-year-old brother, Andrew, was sprawled on the floor with his nose buried deep in a kung fu magazine.

"Hi, Andrew. Merry Christmas," said Julie.

"Uh-huh," said Andrew, not taking his eyes off the page.

"Look, Joo-hee," said Missy, holding up a miniature tea set she had gotten for Christmas. "Can we have a tea party?"

"In a little while," said Ivy. "Go ask Po Po to help you set it up."

Just hearing Ivy mention her grandmother sent a sharp pang through Julie. Were Mom and Grandma baking cookies right now, without her?

The two girls plunked down in front of the tall tree, decorated with lots of shiny colored balls and blinking lights. The gingery smell of Mrs. Ling's special pancakes wafted in from the kitchen. *Dad's house seems drab and dreary compared to Ivy's,* thought Julie.

"Your tree is so pretty," said Julie, leaning back to admire it.

"Yours must be pretty, too," said Ivy, "with all the colored lights and ornaments and tinsel."

"Not this year," said Julie.

"Really?" Ivy asked.

"It's a long story," said Julie. She told Ivy about the tears and tension of the last two days.

"Oh," said Ivy. "I thought having two Christmases would be twice as good as one."

"Think again," said Julie.

"Well, around here, it's not so great either," Ivy assured her friend. "Missy got into the new markers Andrew gave me for Christmas and decided to color the bathtub. I had to wipe down all the tile, and Andrew had to scrub around the tub with a toothbrush! It was almost as bad as when we have to clean the whole house for Chinese New Year."

Julie smiled. She knew that Ivy was just trying to make her feel better. "But you love Chinese New Year," said Julie.

"Yes, but we don't love all the cleaning." Ivy handed Julie a tall box wrapped in snowflake paper. "Here—this'll make you feel better."

"Thanks," said Julie. She tore off the wrapping. Through the plastic window of the box, a Chinese doll with rose-red cheeks and shiny black hair smiled back at her.

"Oh, she's beautiful!" Julie whispered, carefully taking the doll out of the box and hugging her. "And this dress looks like real silk."

She smoothed her hand across a turquoise dress shimmering with delicate vines and blossoms. "She's just like your doll, Li Ming."

"Her name's Yue Yan," said Ivy. "It means happy and beautiful."

"That's the perfect name for you," Julie told her doll.

Ivy raced back to her room to get her own doll. Li Ming was wearing a red silk dress. The two girls nestled the dolls in their laps while Ivy reached for her present.

"Open it," Julie urged.

Ivy's brown eyes sparkled when she saw the small pillow Julie had made for her. The fabric had a green-leafed ivy pattern, and in the center Julie had embroidered Ivy's name in Chinese characters. "You made this?" Ivy cried. "How did you know my name in Chinese?"

"Easy," said Julie. "I asked your mom last time I was here, and she drew the characters for me."

"Thank you!" Ivy said. "Let's go put it on my bed right now."

"Then can you show me some more Chinese writing?" Julie asked. "I like making the characters."

"Sure. Wait till you see my new calligraphy set."

Julie sat cross-legged on the floor of Ivy's room while Ivy took out a satin-lined box that held her brush-and-ink set. She showed Julie how to hold the brush with the pointed tip. "Hold it straight up and down, not like a pencil. Here, I'll show you how to write your name in Chinese." Ivy put a few drops of water in a small blue-and-white-porcelain dish and swirled the ink stick in it, making a rich black ink. The girls practiced on the pages of an old phone book.

"My brush strokes look so messy!" Julie said.

"Try less ink," said Ivy. "And don't press so hard."

Julie's brush strokes were too heavy, and then too wiggly. At last, she got the two characters of her name to look the way Ivy had drawn them.

"That's good!" said Ivy.

"What does yours say?" Julie asked, pointing to Ivy's lettering.

"It means 'double happiness,'" said Ivy.

"I never knew you could letter so well in Chinese," Julie said.

"I learned it in Chinese school," Ivy told her.

"We'll practice more later. Let's clean up and play with our dolls."

"Where's Tracy?" Julie asked when she got back to Dad's house. "Is she still up in her room? Do you think she'll come down?"

"She went back to Mom's today, honey," Dad told her. "Your mother's back from Santa Rosa, and Tracy just wasn't happy here."

"But I thought—"

"It's okay. I want her to feel like this is her home, too. But for now, I think it's best to give her some space. It can take time to heal the hurt from something as painful as a divorce."

Julie nodded. "I know, Dad."

For the rest of the week, Julie and Dad shot hoops every day, sun or rain, and made dinner together every night. Besides getting to spend time with Dad, Julie loved having Ivy so close—a whole week to be right across the street from her best friend. All week, they played with their dolls, practiced Chinese calligraphy with Ivy's brush-and-ink set, and roller-skated or rode their bikes when it wasn't raining.

Before she knew it, the holiday week was over, and Julie was saying good-bye to Ivy. "I wish Christmas break would last forever," Julie said.

"I'm going to miss you," said Ivy, hugging her. "But don't worry, we'll still see each other on the weekends you're here, right?"

Julie nodded, blinking back tears. She never seemed to get used to saying good-bye to her friend. Clutching her doll to her, she ran through the light rain to Dad's house.

GOOD FORTUNE

When Julie got back to Mom's house, it was January. Hank had already taken away the Christmas tree, and the ornaments were carefully put away. Julie tried her best to return to regular life, but she couldn't shake a hollow, unsettled feeling. As happy as she was to be back with Mom, there was still that empty place inside her, missing Dad.

After school each day, Julie read and reread her new books, put her jigsaw puzzle together for the second time, and knitted a hat and scarf for Yue Yan with her new knitting kit from Tracy. When she found herself feeling lonely, she thought of Ivy. Lucky Ivy! She had her whole family around her,

plus a special celebration, Chinese New Year,
to look forward to.

Two weeks passed slowly, and then it was
mid-January, and Julie was back at Dad's for the
weekend. As usual, Tracy had refused to come.

Julie was just about to knock on Ivy's front door
when it opened.

"Oh, hi, Mrs. Ling!" Ivy's mom usually wore
a straight skirt and pretty vest, and her hair always
had a just-brushed look. But today, the slender
Mrs. Ling was wearing an oversized man's shirt,
and her smooth black hair was hidden under
a scarf.

"Julie! Come in. I was just going to shake out
this rug. As you can see, we've been doing some
cleaning. Only two weeks till Chinese New Year!"

Missy followed Mrs. Ling, pretending to sweep
with a child-sized broom. "Out with the old and in
with the new!" she said in a sing-song voice.

Ivy appeared, holding an ink brush. "Come on up
to my room. You can help me make some banners."

"Have you finished cleaning all the downstairs
windows?" Mrs. Ling asked.

"Almost," said Ivy.

"Windows first," said Mrs. Ling.

"I can help," Julie offered. One by one, Julie sprayed the windows in the front room, and Ivy followed close behind, wiping them clean.

"Thanks for helping," said Ivy. "Cleaning goes way faster with two."

"Yeah, but now we smell like salad," said Julie.

"It's from the vinegar in the spray bottle," said Ivy, laughing. "Let's go up to my room and I'll show you how to write the characters for *Gung Hay Fat Choy.*"

"What does that mean?" asked Julie as the girls sat down at Ivy's desk.

"Good luck and good health in the new year," Ivy translated. She dipped her brush in the little dish of ink and began painting characters with a few sure, quick strokes.

 Julie held her brush straight and made a Chinese character that looked a bit like an umbrella with raindrops. "You're really getting the hang of this," said Ivy. "Hey, maybe we can make a banner to hang by the door. You should see the banners Po Po made when she wasn't much older than me.

They're the ones we bring out every year for New Year's. Each one has a Chinese poem. I'm trying to copy Po Po's brush strokes." Ivy unrolled several long scrolls of paper, telling Julie what each poem said:

> *Springtime*
> *New shoots grow*
> *Taller by the spreading*
> *Rays of the sun*
>
> *Make a candle*
> *To bring brightness*
> *Read a book*
> *To achieve learning*

"Wow," Julie said with admiration. "Look, this Chinese character even looks like a seed pushing up out of the ground."

Ivy nodded. "The next time you come, we'll hang these up on the wall to decorate the house for Chinese New Year."

Julie couldn't wait till her next week at Dad's. After breakfast with Dad, she hurried over to her friend's house.

"Ivy! You got your hair cut!" cried Julie as Ivy opened the door.

"Mama says it's good fortune to cut your hair before the New Year. Cut off the old and start new. What do you think?" Ivy blew a puff of air to ruffle her new bangs.

"It's great! You look kind of like Nancy Drew with her pageboy haircut."

"Thanks," said Ivy. "Guess what? Today's the Chinatown Flower Fair! The weekend before Chinese New Year, everyone buys flowers and fruits. It's like a street carnival."

"Sounds neat," said Julie. "Are you—are you going there now?" She tried to keep the disappointment out of her voice. Ivy nodded.

Mrs. Ling stood framed in the doorway, holding Missy's hand and calling to Andrew to put his shoes on. "You're welcome to come along, Julie."

Julie's heart lifted. "Just let me go ask my dad!" she called as she raced back across the street.

On their way to Chinatown, Ivy said, "Mama, let's go the long way so that we can enter through the dragon gate." At the entrance to Chinatown, a great green gate crested with golden dragons arched over Grant Avenue. A few blocks later, Ivy pointed out her grandparents restaurant, the Happy Panda.

As they joined the throngs of people crowding the streets, Julie's eyes grew wide with wonder. She had been to Chinatown before, but today the neighborhood was like a city unto itself, bursting with new colors, smells, and sounds. Sidewalk vendors called out in Chinese, their voices dipping and rising like songbirds as they unloaded produce from trucks. Silvery fish stared out of wooden crates labeled with Chinese characters. Racks of bright silks fluttered in the breeze, while lines of laundry flapped from second-story balconies.

The children followed Mrs. Ling up and down Stockton Street. Elbow to elbow, they threaded their way through the crowds, past cardboard boxes brimming with wrinkly vegetables and prickly fruits.

"What are all these?" asked Julie.

 "Chinese cabbage, wood ear mushrooms, and bitter melon," Ivy told her, pointing at each vegetable.

"How are you ever going to eat all this?" asked Julie as Ivy's mom began to load them up with bags of food.

"Don't worry, we will," said Ivy. "Chinese New Year lasts for fifteen days! It starts on New Year's Eve with a big family dinner at home. It ends with a feast at the Happy Panda on the night of the dragon parade—"

"—which *I'm* going to be in!" Andrew piped up. "And it's time for me to go to practice. See you later!"

"No fair," said Ivy. "We need you to help carry bags!"

"That's what you have Julie for," Andrew teased, waving and heading off toward the Chinatown Y.

"We can't forget tangerines, for good luck," Ivy told Julie. "Look for tangerines that still have stems with leaves attached. That's for friendship, and staying connected."

Julie carefully selected a tangerine with a firm stem and two green leaves. She thought about her own family, about Tracy and Dad. *If only it were that easy to stay connected.*

Soon Julie and Ivy were weighed down with pink plastic bags brimming with fruits and vegetables. Mrs. Ling piled them even higher with peach blossoms, peonies, and chrysanthemums.

"Peach blossoms are for long life, and good luck, too," Ivy said.

"We need good luck," said Julie. "Good luck carrying all this stuff home!"

Mrs. Ling paused outside a souvenir shop to talk to a woman in a red quilted jacket. Ivy and Julie set their bags down, waiting while the women spoke rapidly in Chinese.

"Hey, Ivy, is the doll shop anywhere around here?" Julie asked, looking up and down the street.

"It's just past the kite shop, a few doors down."

"Do we have time to look in the window?"

"Sure," said Ivy, glancing at her mother and the souvenir-shop lady. "They'll be talking for about a million years."

Pushing through the crowds, the girls gazed into the storefront window. "Wow," said Julie. "They have doll dresses and dollhouses and miniature furniture. Let's go inside!"

A bell jangled as they opened the door. The shop was like an attic crammed full of treasure. Jade princess dolls. Dragon tea sets, drums, and fans. Traditional Chinese papercuts. Lion masks and lanterns. Satin dresses and pajamas.

"Look," said Ivy. "They have Chinese dresses in girls' sizes. Let's try them on."

Julie lifted a turquoise dress from the rack that looked very much like Yue Yan's dress. It felt silky-smooth to the touch. "If I had a dress this fancy, I'd ask Dad to take me back to the Fairmont Hotel. Only this time, Tracy wouldn't be there to ruin it."

Ivy selected a red dress like Li Ming's. "If I had a dress this fancy, I'd wear it for New Year's!" she said.

The girls tugged the dresses on over their clothes. They whirled and twirled in front of the long mirror. "Wish to buy?" asked the saleslady, smiling.

The girls tugged the dresses on over their clothes. They whirled and twirled in front of the long mirror.

"Not today, thank you," Ivy said politely.

The girls reluctantly hung the dresses up and hurried back outside. They ran past the kite shop, a Chinese bakery, and an herb shop. But when they got to the souvenir shop, Mrs. Ling and Missy were nowhere in sight. Even their bags were gone.

Ivy and Julie looked up and down the sidewalk, inside the souvenir shop, and across the street. "Mama!" Ivy called out, trying to see above the crowd. "Mama! Where are you?"

"It's my fault," said Julie frantically. "We shouldn't have gone inside that shop. We took too long. They could be anywhere!"

"But Mama wouldn't leave without us!" Ivy went back into the souvenir shop to ask the shopkeeper if she knew which way her mother and sister had gone. The woman replied in rapid Chinese. Ivy's face fell.

"She says they went to find us," she told Julie.

"Okay," said Julie, taking a deep breath. "Think, Ivy, if your mom was looking for us, where would she go?" Ivy closed her eyes for a minute. "I know! She must have gone to the fortune-cookie factory. Remember? She said that was her last stop."

"Do you know how to get there?" Julie asked.

"It can't be too far from here. I know it's in a little alley, next to a barbershop. C'mon. Hurry!"

Julie and Ivy bent low and ducked through the crowds filling the sidewalk. When they turned the corner, the crowds thinned out a bit. They rushed down a few blocks, searching in every direction. Nothing looked familiar. Julie's heart quickened. She felt lost in a foreign country. Even the words people spoke were impossible to understand.

Ivy made a sharp turn into an alley where the tall backs of buildings blocked the sunlight. A cascade of overturned boxes littered the alley. Heaps of cabbage leaves were scattered every which way.

"Pee-yew! This place smells!" Julie held her nose. "Are you sure this is it?"

"No," said Ivy, her voice cracking. "I'm not sure."

"Let's try the next alley," said Julie. Somehow, as long as they kept moving, it didn't seem so scary.

As they entered the narrow alley, crumbling brick walls hemmed them in. Julie gripped Ivy's hand. An old man came up to them, pointing his cane and muttering in Chinese.

"What's he saying?" Julie whispered.

"I don't know. C'mon, let's get out of here."

"Wait! Listen—what's that strange noise?" Julie asked.

"What noise?"

"That clickety-clackety sound. It sounds like rain on a tin roof."

Ivy stopped to listen. Her eyes lit up. "Those are mah-jongg tiles! It's a game Gung Gung plays." Ivy craned her neck, looking up to the second story of the old brick building. "This looks just like the place where Gung Gung plays. If he's up there, he can help us find Mama and Missy."

mah-jongg tiles

Taking two steps at a time, Julie followed Ivy up the iron staircase to a long open room lined with tables, where Chinese men were clustered in small groups, slapping down ivory-colored tiles that sounded like dominoes. *Clickety-clack, clickety-clack.*

"Do you see him, Ivy?" Julie asked. "Is he here?"

"Gung Gung!" Ivy called, rushing over to her grandfather. "We need your help."

As Ivy explained what had happened, Gung Gung rose from his table, spoke in Chinese to the other men, and beckoned the girls to follow him. He led them back down the iron staircase into the alley below and pointed to a brick building down the block.

A warm, sugary-sweet smell filled Julie's nose. "Yum—I smell pancakes. Or maybe French toast."

"That's the fortune-cookie factory! I smell it, too," Ivy said, sniffing the air. "Now I know where we are. Thanks, Gung Gung." Her grandfather's face crinkled into a smile as he guided the girls toward the fortune-cookie factory.

As soon as she saw Ivy's mom, Julie felt her whole body relax.

"Mama!" called Ivy, running up to hug her.

"Oh, Ivy, you girls scared me half to death!" Mrs. Ling said. "I turned around and you had disappeared. All I could think was that maybe you'd gone ahead to the cookie factory."

"I'm sorry, Mama," said Ivy, hanging her head.

"It's all my fault," said Julie. "I wanted to go inside the doll shop."

"But you're the one who heard the mah-jongg tiles," Ivy said. "If it weren't for you, we might not have found Gung Gung, and we'd still be lost."

"Well, we're all found now," said Gung Gung, putting his arms around Ivy and Julie. Missy hugged them, too. "And I have a mah-jongg game to finish." The girls waved as he turned to go.

Mrs. Ling shook her head, looking more relieved than angry. "Now, no more wandering away, please. This is not the day to get lost in Chinatown."

"We know, Mama," said Ivy as they followed the heavenly smell into the fortune-cookie factory.

Two women sat in front of machines that looked like gigantic waffle irons. Each machine poured out small circles of batter, and the women folded each circle into a half-moon fortune-cookie shape, slipping a secret fortune inside with one swift motion. The women spoke to Mrs. Ling in Chinese, and then handed each girl a fresh, warm fortune cookie.

Mrs. Ling told the girls, "Look inside for a happy new year fortune."

Ivy broke her fortune cookie in half and pulled out the small slip of paper.

"What does it say?" asked Julie between bites.

"'A new blade of grass pushes through earth to reach the sun.' How about yours?" asked Ivy.

"Mine's funny. It says, 'New beginnings are like new shoes.'"

"I don't get it," said Ivy. "How is a new beginning like a new shoe?"

Julie thought for a minute. "Well," she said, "new shoes pinch and give you blisters . . ."

"So we're going to get a lot of blisters in the new year? I'm not sure I like that fortune."

Julie looked at both fortunes as she munched the rest of her cookie. "I think," she said slowly, "they're both saying it's not always easy when you first start something new."

GUNG HAY FAT CHOY

"Julie," Tracy called. "Phone's for you!"

"Alley Oop? It's me, Ivy. Did you get it? Did you get my invitation to the Happy Panda for Chinese New Year?"

"Mom showed it to me as soon as I got home from school," said Julie. "We're coming for sure!"

"Mama said you've been such a big help getting ready for Chinese New Year that we could invite your whole family," Ivy bubbled.

"You mean my—my *whole* family?" Julie asked, the words sticking in her throat.

"Sure. I already took an invitation over to your Dad, and he said he'd love to come. Did you know it's the Year of the Dragon?"

Julie swallowed. Thinking about Tracy and Dad

together in the same room was like coming face-to-face with her *own* dragon.

"I can't wait," Ivy went on. "This'll be the best Chinese New Year ever!"

Julie hung up the phone, biting her fingernail. She wished she could share Ivy's excitement. But all she could feel was worry, and the worry turned to dread every time she pictured her whole family together in the same room. What if Tracy got upset with Dad and made another scene that would embarrass Julie in front of the Lings? She couldn't bear to think about another ruined holiday. Chinese New Year was all about good fortune and family togetherness. Right now her family didn't have much of either.

Julie bit another nail, feeling guilty. She knew she should be looking forward to the Chinese New Year celebration with Ivy and her family. *Maybe it would be simpler if I just didn't go,* she thought. But then she'd be letting Ivy down, not to mention herself.

Families sure were complicated! Julie didn't remember things being so confusing before her parents split up. She felt a nervous knot in her chest, ten times worse than when she and Ivy were lost in Chinatown.

"Julie," Mom said, coming into the kitchen, "you're going to wear those nails down to the nub. Is something wrong? Everything okay at school?"

Julie collapsed into a chair. "School's fine, Mom. I'm just—just worried about something."

"Maybe I can help," Mom offered.

Julie looked at Mom, and in a few short minutes, she'd spilled out the whole dilemma. Just telling Mom eased the tight knot inside her.

Mom gently rubbed her back. "Oh, Julie, I'm glad you told me. I hate to see you hold so much in."

"I know, Mom, but it has to do with what happened at Dad's over Christmas, and I wasn't sure I should be talking to you about that."

"Christmas was hard for all of us this year. Just remember, if it has to do with our family, you can always come to me."

Julie nodded, her throat tight.

"As hard as it is being apart, it's not always easy being together either, is it," Mom went on. "And we're going to run into this the rest of our lives, honey. Every time there's an important event—not just Christmas, but birthdays, graduations, even weddings—we're going to face this. Maybe this Chinese New Year celebration is a chance for the four of us to practice being together."

"You think so?" asked Julie hopefully.

"I know so," said Mom, planting a kiss on her forehead.

The night of the dragon parade finally arrived. Julie knocked on Ivy's front door. "Alley Oop!" said Ivy. "Gung Hay Fat Choy! Happy New Year!"

"Gung Hay Fat Choy to you, too," said Julie.

Ivy's brown eyes sparkled. "I thought you'd never get here. I'm so excited I can hardly breathe!"

"I wasn't sure what to bring to wear tonight," Julie said, holding up a brown grocery bag that had her red velvet jumper inside.

"C'mon, I want to show you something," Ivy said, pulling Julie back to her room. "Ta-da!" Ivy pointed to a red silk dress laid out on her bed.

"That's the same dress you tried on in Chinatown that day!"

"Can you believe it? It's tradition to wear new clothes for Chinese New Year, and Mama got this for me to wear."

"You're *so* lucky," said Julie. "How'd your mom know?"

Mrs. Ling poked her head into the bedroom. "Mothers know these things," she said with a twinkle.

"It helps if the lady at the shop is your friend," said Ivy, laughing. "And Mama knew this dress matched Li Ming's." Then Ivy went to her closet and pulled out a hanger. Julie gasped. It held the turquoise dress. "It's for you," said Ivy. "Try it on!"

Julie reached out to touch the dress. The silk felt as smooth as rose petals. "It's beautiful," said Julie. "You mean I can wear this tonight?"

"The dress is yours to keep," said Mrs. Ling. "To thank you for all your hard work."

"Oh," Julie said breathlessly. "Thank you so much!" She held the dress up to her neck and spun around the room, then fell on the bed next to Ivy, dizzy and laughing.

Mrs. Ling looked at her watch. "Girls, I'll take the dresses to the restaurant. It's time for us to go."

"Double happiness!" said Ivy, putting her arm around her friend.

❖

When they got to the Happy Panda, Po Po greeted them wearing a purple quilted jacket with fancy knots for buttons. Ivy's grandmother was a tiny woman whose whole face grew rounder when she smiled. Today her salt-and-pepper hair was pinned up with red cinnabar hair sticks.

Po Po showed the girls how to set the tables, fold the napkins into fans, and fill all eight sections of the *chuen-hop*, the traditional Tray of Togetherness, with candied fruits and red melon seeds.

"Careful," warned Po Po. "Bad luck to break a dish!"

Julie and Ivy were especially careful with the gold-rimmed plates. When they were finished, each large round table glittered, a kaleidoscope of red and gold. Crystal glasses glinted in the late afternoon sun.

Julie and Ivy hurried to the back office to slip on their new dresses. Ivy gave Julie a pair of embroidered Chinese slippers to wear.

Mrs. Ling came to the door. "You girls are as pretty as a picture," she said. "Come on out and let everyone admire you!"

❀

People began streaming into the Happy Panda—Ivy's aunts, uncles, cousins, and friends of the family—calling "Happy New Year!" and "Gung Hay Fat Choy!" Everyone brought hostess gifts for Po Po and Mrs. Ling, and, for all the children, lucky red envelopes called *lai see*.

"Each one has a dollar bill inside," Ivy explained. "Don't tell Andrew, but I played a joke on him and put Monopoly money inside one of his envelopes!" The two girls giggled, imagining the look on Andrew's face when he opened the envelope.

Soon Julie's dad arrived. He handed Mrs. Ling a box of candy. "It's marzipan in the shape of animals—my holiday favorite as a boy," he told her.

Julie grinned, delighted that Dad had known to bring a gift. Mrs. Ling accepted the box with a gracious nod. "Welcome!" she said. "Welcome to the Happy Panda."

Mr. Ling came over to shake Dad's hand. "We're so glad you could come."

"Thank you for inviting me," said Dad. "I haven't been to a Chinese banquet like this since I was in China back in 1971."

"How did you manage that?" asked Mr. Ling, his dark eyebrows raised with curiosity. "Travel to China was banned for Americans."

"Just happened to be in the right place at the right time," Dad replied. "I had flown the U.S. table tennis team to Japan, when they unexpectedly got invited to China. I was asked to be a backup pilot on the charter flight from Tokyo to Peking."

"No kidding," said Mr. Ling, raking back his short black hair. "I remember we all had great hopes for President Nixon's Ping-Pong diplomacy."

"What's Ping-Pong diplomacy?" asked Julie.

"That's when China first renewed friendship with the United States after many years of political disagreement," Mr. Ling explained.

Ivy tugged Julie's arm. "There's your mom and sister."

Mom greeted Mrs. Ling, handing her a delicate purple orchid. "It's great to see our old neighbors," Mom said. She turned to Julie, holding her at arm's length. "Oh my—let me look at you!"

"Jules, you look fab in that Chinese dress," Tracy gushed.

"Thanks," said Julie, breathing a sigh of relief that Tracy seemed to be in a good mood.

Gung Gung tapped a chopstick against a water glass. "Honored guests," he said when everyone quieted down, "we are so happy and blessed to have you all come together with us for this special New Year's feast.

"When my father first came to this country, life wasn't easy. San Francisco seemed new and strange, so different from China and all he left behind. He had to make a fresh start. After years of hard work, he opened a restaurant, the Happy Panda. And here we are today, many years later, celebrating Chinese New Year—in America!"

Everybody clapped. Mr. Ling added, "Please, everyone, find your seat at one of the tables, and let us begin our meal. Gung Hay Fat Choy. Happy New Year to you all."

The first course was soup. Tracy peered into the bowl of murky brown broth. "What is it?" she whispered to Julie.

"Shh!" Julie whispered. "Please just eat it. It's rude not to appreciate the food."

"I've never had authentic bird's nest soup before," Dad said.

"Bird's nest soup? You didn't tell me I'd be eating a bird's nest!" Tracy whispered back to Julie.

"Just try it, Tracy," Julie urged softly.

Tracy took a hesitant sip. "Mmm, this is actually pretty good."

"See? Trying new things is not so bad," said Julie.

As soon as the soup bowls were cleared, trays of bright green vegetables, platters of glistening fish and chicken, and steaming bowls of rice and noodles were brought to the table.

"Long-life noodles," Po Po told the guests. "Okay to slurp. Very bad luck to cut noodles!"

"I've never seen so many colorful plates of food!" Mom said.

"Smells delicious, too," said Dad.

For a few minutes, all Julie could hear was

the clicking of chopsticks. Dad kept dropping a dumpling onto his plate. Julie hoped none of the Lings had seen.

"No matter how many times I've tried eating with chopsticks, I still can't quite get the hang of it," Dad said.

"Try keeping the bottom one still, and just move the top one," Tracy suggested, turning toward Dad for the first time that evening and clicking her own chopsticks in the air to show him how.

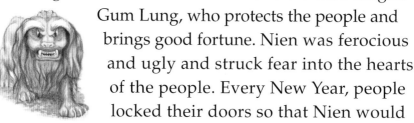

"Hey, that really works!" said Dad, trying it out.

When the meal was finished and everyone was sipping tea and chatting, Gung Gung announced, "Time for a story! Tonight's tale goes back to the olden days in China, when the monster Nien came down out of the mountains and scared all the villagers. This monster was not like the wise dragon Gum Lung, who protects the people and brings good fortune. Nien was ferocious and ugly and struck fear into the hearts of the people. Every New Year, people locked their doors so that Nien would

the monster Nien

58

not come gobble them up.

"One year, a wise old man gathered the people together and told them to bring drums and gongs and noisemakers of every kind to scare the beast away.

"The next time Nien appeared, the people were ready. They beat drums and lit firecrackers. Never before had there been such a furious noise, and the monster Nien fled back into the mountains, never to be seen again. So each year, we beat drums, clang cymbals, and light firecrackers in our parade to make sure the monster Nien never returns!"

Missy peeked out from behind her hands. "Is the scary story over, Gung Gung?"

"Yes," said Gung Gung, his face crinkling into a smile. "But the parade is about to begin."

At least Tracy didn't make a scene, Julie thought to herself. But she could still feel a lump of disappointment in her chest. The dinner was over, and other than showing him how to use chopsticks, Tracy had avoided talking to Dad. The celebration hadn't exactly brought them together.

"Tracy, can't you be nicer to Dad?" Julie whispered, looking around to make sure no one else could hear.

"What do you mean?" asked Tracy. "I didn't say anything."

"That's just the point! You didn't even try to talk to him."

"I don't know what to say to him."

"Tracy, it's *Dad.* Just be yourself—talk about anything. School, or tennis—it doesn't matter what. C'mon, give him a chance. He just wants to be part of your life. Why can't you let him?"

Tracy glanced over at Dad. He stood sipping the last of his tea, studying a painting of a lone cypress hanging on the back wall of the restaurant. "I'll try," said Tracy in a soft voice.

Up on the iron balcony above the Happy Panda, Julie and her family had a bird's-eye view of the Chinatown streets below. Throngs of people jammed the sidewalks. Bright banners fluttered outside every shop, colorful paper lanterns swayed in the night breeze, and firecrackers popped in the distance.

"What a view from up here," Dad remarked. "I don't know when I've enjoyed myself so much."

"And I don't know when I've eaten so much!" Mom joked.

Tracy leaned over to whisper in Julie's ear. "Guess what, Jules. I invited Dad to my tennis match next week."

"What did he say?" Julie asked.

"He's going to come," said Tracy.

"Didn't I tell you?" Julie smiled.

They heard a thunderous *boom, boom, boom,* and the first drums of the parade went by. There were glittering floats, marching bands, acrobats, and stilt walkers. A blizzard of red confetti from all the firecrackers floated through the air like snowflakes, and clouds of smoke puffed skyward. Missy clapped her hands as the lion dancers dipped and bowed inside their white-whiskered, lion-headed costumes.

lion dancers

"Where's Gum Lung, Po Po?" Missy asked.

"Dragon will come at the end," said Po Po. "Must be patient."

"There's Andrew!" called Ivy. "Look, I see him. Wave to Andrew, Missy."

"Dragon!" shouted Missy. "Dragon, dragon!"

Right in front of the dragon's head, Andrew whirled a red ball on a long stick. The crowds went wild as Gum Lung, the great dragon, weaved its way through the streets, dipping its head, blinking its eyes, and clacking its giant mouth. The onlookers erupted in cries and applause. Missy covered her ears.

"Gung Hay Fat Choy," Po Po said above the noise. "A new year begins."

Julie thought back to how Ivy's great-grandfather had left behind his home, his family, and everything he knew to come to America and make a fresh start. Just a few short months ago, she too had felt as if she were leaving behind everything she once knew, moving to a whole new life. She'd been filled with her own fears about the divorce, about moving, about her family splitting apart.

But now, thinking about the journey Ivy's great-grandfather had taken filled her with hope for new beginnings. Tonight, even Tracy and Dad were making a new start. This night had shown that her family could come together in celebration, and Julie was happy for that.

The firecrackers died down and lingering wisps

Gum Lung, the great dragon, weaved its way through the streets.

of smoke drifted like fog out toward the bay. As the last marching band passed by below, the clanging of cymbals and banging of drums reminded Julie of Gung Gung's story—how the people in Old China had made loud noises to drive away their fears. Julie held up the noisemaker Ivy had given her and twirled it. She smiled as the echoing sound rang out into the night.

LOOKING BACK

HOLIDAY
TRADITIONS
IN THE
1970s

American families experienced many changes in their society in the 1970s, but they cherished their holiday traditions and celebrated Christmas much as they always had. Girls who lived in big cities enjoyed attending the Nutcracker ballet and other special holiday performances, just as they do today. Fancy downtown hotels had elaborate decorations and served special holiday meals, like the Nutcracker tea Julie went to at the Fairmont.

Families have always enjoyed making holiday decorations, and in the 1970s, handmade decorations reached new heights of popularity. People liked to use found materials for their handcrafts, especially natural materials such as seedpods and dried beans.

Ornaments made out of dried milkweed pods

For children with divorced parents, the holidays did change in one important way: instead of whole families gathering together, the children often spent Christmas with only one parent and one side of their family. If they spent part of the holiday with the other parent, they might have Christmas twice, as Julie did. Nowadays, many children divide their holidays this way, but in Julie's time, it was much less common.

Dividing the Christmas holiday between her parents was hard for Julie, and she found comfort in the Chinese holiday traditions that Ivy's family practiced. Chinese New Year is a 15-day celebration that begins on the first new moon of the year and ends on the full moon. Families prepare for the holiday by settling debts and disagreements, buying new clothes, and scrubbing their homes from top to bottom. Then they decorate with fresh flowers and hang good wishes for the new year, written in

Shopping at San Francisco's Flower Fair for Chinese New Year

A young girl learning Chinese calligraphy

Chinese, on red paper throughout their home. The wishes tend to be more general than new year's resolutions—typical wishes are for happiness, wealth, a long life, and good fortune.

Many families also hang spring *couplets,* or short poems, in their homes, as Ivy's family did.

During Chinese New Year, the color red is considered good luck. People wear new outfits that often have a little red—or a lot—in the design. Young girls often wear pink. Red candles are burned, and children get *lai see*, red envelopes with money in them, from their elders. The lucky

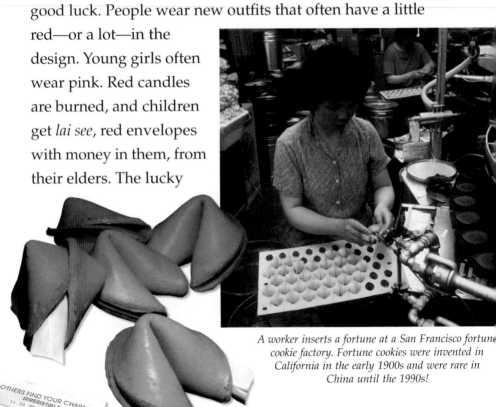

A worker inserts a fortune at a San Francisco fortune cookie factory. Fortune cookies were invented in California in the early 1900s and were rare in China until the 1990s!

OTHERS FIND YOUR CHARM
IRRESISTIBLE
11 23 30 35 40

red envelopes are supposed to bring good fortune to the giver as well as the receiver.

The New Year's Eve dinner is the most important family ritual of the year for Chinese Americans. Chinese restaurants often close for the evening while families gather with relatives and friends for their year-end holiday feast. Conflicts are set aside, and families remember and honor their ancestors, much the way Gung Gung remembered his father at the banquet.

red envelope for money

Girls in traditional Chinese costumes march in a Chinese New Year parade. They are playing bell lyras, a marching-band instrument.

In San Francisco, as in other cities with a large Chinese American population, the holiday ends with a big parade. San Francisco's is the oldest and largest Chinese New Year parade in the United States, and the entire community turns out for the event. There are lavishly decorated floats, martial arts groups, and school marching bands. The parade also features Chinese acrobats, stilt walkers, and troupes of lion dancers. Lion dancing is an ancient art form that was performed at important festivals in China. Today, lion dancers are popular in Chinese New Year parades and other festivities throughout the United States.

In San Francisco, the streets of Chinatown are packed during Chinese New Year.

A lion dancer costume

The parade ends with the grand finale—the Golden Dragon, accompanied by the loud popping of 600,000 firecrackers! The dragon itself is over 200 feet long and is carried by a team of 100 people. To be part of the grand finale, like Ivy's brother, Andrew, is a great honor.

Chinese New Year celebrates togetherness and new beginnings. It is a time when families reflect on the past and look forward to making a fresh start in the new year. For Julie, the Chinese New Year celebration was a perfect opportunity to think deeply about how things had changed in her family—and how she could help make her family relationships as good as possible in the coming year.

A SNEAK PEEK AT

Julie

AND THE EAGLES

One spring day, Julie and Ivy hear a mysterious noise in the park. It turns out to be a baby bird—and it needs help.

What's that noise?" Julie asked, looking around.

"That's me slurping my snow cone," said Ivy.

"No, I mean that little squeak. Hear it?" Both girls craned their necks toward the grove of trees behind their bench.

"There—look," said Julie, jumping up. "I saw something move under that pink bush." The girls stood as still as statues. They did not hear a peep.

"Maybe we scared it," said Julie.

Weep, weep.

Julie looked at Ivy. Ivy looked at Julie. Their eyes grew wide. "There it is again," Julie whispered.

"I heard it, too," Ivy said.

"Sounds like a baby bird," said Julie. The girls peered under the azalea bush. Julie blinked. A pair of round yellow eyes blinked back at her.

"A baby owl!" she whispered. It was no bigger than a tennis ball, with pointy ear tufts and a sharp hooked beak. It was covered with downy gray fuzz as soft as dandelion fluff.

"Where's your mama?" Ivy asked.

"Maybe it's hurt," said Julie. "It must have fallen

out of a nest. It's too young to fly." She peered up at the treetops, looking for a nest. "I don't see anything that looks like a nest."

"Even if we did find a nest, how would we get the baby back up into it?" Ivy asked. "And I don't hear a mama owl calling."

"All I hear are those noisy crows," said Julie, glancing at the black birds circling overhead. "They might come after it. We have to save it."

"Can't the mama owl come save it?" Ivy asked.

"What if it's lost? We can't just leave it here—a cat or a dog or a raccoon could find it." Julie untied her sweatshirt from around her waist. She turned it inside out to make a soft bed and set it under the bush next to the owl. "C'mon, little one," she coaxed. "Hop into my sweatshirt and we'll take you home."

The baby bird didn't move.

"Something's wrong with it," said Ivy.

Cupping her hand under the baby owl, Julie lifted it into the soft sweatshirt and eased it out from under the bush. The girls stood a moment, in awe of the small creature.

"Don't be scared," Julie whispered. "We'll take care of you." Carefully, she settled the bird in the

basket on the front of her bike. The baby
owl nestled down into the folds, as if it
were being tucked into bed.

"Aw, he's sooooo cute!" said Ivy.
"Look at all that soft, fluffy fuzz."

"Let's get you home, fuzz face," Julie cooed. She
hopped on her bike and was just about to push off
when she froze. "Wait a minute. We can't take it to
my apartment. There's no pets allowed. You'll have
to take it home to your house."

"I can't," said Ivy. "We have two cats, remember?
The bird would last about two seconds around
Jasmine and Won Ton."

"And I can't take it to Dad's house, since I'm
only there on weekends, and he's away a lot." Julie
twisted the hem of her shirt, thinking.

Ivy grabbed Julie's arm and pointed. "Look,
there's that nice lady who told us about the
butterflies. Maybe she knows about birds, too."

"Good idea," said Julie. They wheeled their bikes
across the grass to the lady, who was bent over
sniffing a bright red azalea.

"Excuse me," said Julie.

The woman looked up. "Oh, hello again, girls."

"We found a baby owl," said Julie, parting the folds of her sweatshirt to show the lady. "We heard it crying. We couldn't find its mother or see a nest and we thought we shouldn't leave it there all alone, but we don't know what to do."

"Looks to me like you've found a baby screech owl. They don't build nests—they live in holes in trees."

"No wonder we couldn't see any nest," said Ivy.

"Poor thing's trembling," said the woman. "It must have fallen out of a tree."

"What should we do?" Julie asked.

"It needs help right away," the lady said. "Do you girls know where the Randall Museum is? It's not far from the park. They have a rescue center there. They can take care of injured wild animals."

"It's just a few blocks from my house," said Julie. "I've passed by there lots of times."

"I'm sure they'll know what to do," said the lady.

"Thanks," Julie and Ivy called, hopping back on their bikes. Julie cooed to the little owl all the way out of the park, down Waller Street, and up the hill to the museum.